The Pond of Reflection

Written by
Catherine Ann Russell

Illustrated by
Brooke Connor

Book One in The Pearls of Wisdom Series:
Stories Inspired by a Biblical Proverb

The Pond of Reflection by Catherine Ann Russell
Book 1 in The Pearls of Wisdom Series:
Stories Inspired by a Biblical Proverb

Hardcover ISBN: 978-1-956693-03-4
Paperback ISBN: 978-1-956693-04-1
eBook ISBN: 978-1-956693-05-8

Library of Congress Number: 2021919291

Printed in the United States of America

Basketful Relief Project
POB 994
Lyons, CO 80540
cat@basketfulreliefproject.com

Copyediting by Katie Chambers of Beacon Point Services (beaconpointservices.org)

Cover and interior design by Janell E. Robisch of Speculation Editing (speculationsediting.com)

Illustrations by Brooke Connor of Brooke Connor Design (www.brookeconnordesign.com)

To Wilma, Margot, and Harriet
Each beautiful from the inside-out and the outside-in.

As water reflects the face, so one's life reflects the heart.

Prov 27:19 (NIV)

The Pond of Reflection

The Pond of Reflection is book one in The Pearls of Wisdom Series: Stories Inspired by a Biblical Proverb. It is a children's chapter book written for the Basketful Relief Project (BRP) dedicated to help fund emergency famine relief efforts around the world. The BRP donates gift dollars to established relief organizations from the purchase of this book. To find out more visit: www.basketfulreliefproject.com.

Contents

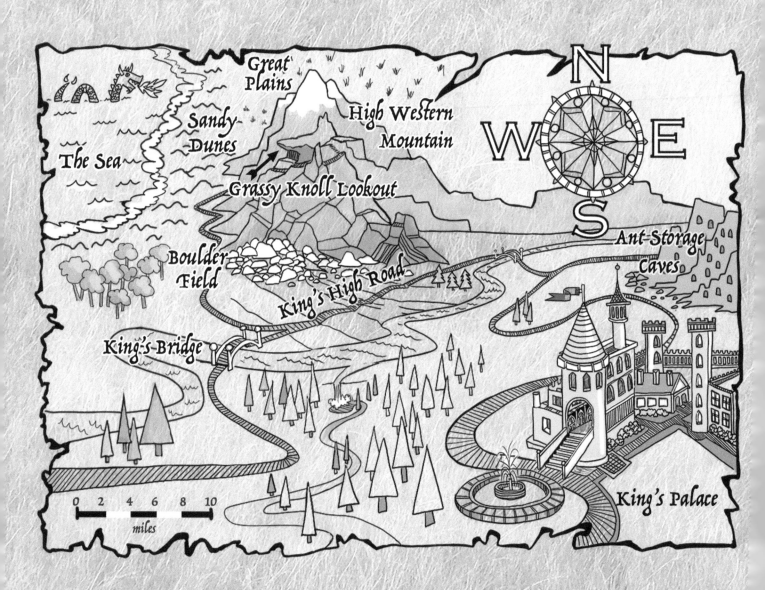

Chapter 1
The Mirrorless Kingdom

Once upon a time, there lived a great king. The king was good and kind, wise and courageous, although one might not think so at first sight. For this king was a mouse, and if it were not for the crown on his head, one might initially mistake him for any other mouse. Being a wise king, however, he knew his heart to be courageous and kind, and so to him what he looked like from the outside-in was not as important as who he knew he was from the inside-out. Being confident on the inside was so important to him that, by his command, no mirrors were allowed in his kingdom. He wanted all creatures in his realm to know their own hearts and to be happy with themselves just as they were.

All the creatures great and small, who lived happily under the king's protection, knew just how good and kind, wise and courageous was their king, for they were all content and celebrated many festive occasions with the king and his court. Each day all enjoyed the goodness of the king's realm, which reached as far as the eye could see. In fact, it reached so far that wherever one found oneself, one was under the king's rule and keeping.

It was a beautiful kingdom, with sprawling forests, glens, meadows, and mountains, and gushing rivers descending to a vast blue ocean.

For ages and ages, all was well in this kingdom, without any creature minding that a mirror could not be found. Bears seemed happy as bears, foxes as foxes, goats as goats, and bees as bees. All but one, that is: the king's daughter.

Yes, the king did have a daughter whom he loved very much, and she, in turn, loved him. She called him Papa, and he called her my daughter, even though her real name was Journee. She was growing up to be like him, for she too was good and kind. However, being so young, she had not yet had the many experiences and adventures that made her father wise about many things. Even so, she was growing up and throwing a coming-of-age birthday party the Saturday next, with the entire kingdom invited to celebrate the grand occasion.

"Papa," Journee asked, "may I have a mirror for my birthday? It would be lovely to know who I am by seeing what I look like to others."

"My daughter," replied the king, "who does your heart say you are?"

Journee hung her head as she replied. "Papa, I'm not so sure of myself. My heart tells me I am good and kind like you. But I might be other things too, and I think perhaps seeing my reflection will help me know who I really am. I see my hands and my feet and the tips of my whiskers, my soft fuzzy tummy, and my tail just like yours. But what if I am not really a mouse but a rat, or a vole, or a gerbil?

"Ah," her father replied with a twinkle in his eye. "I think I would love you just as much if you were a rat or a vole or a gerbil, but alas, you are a mouse like me. Do you think your heart would be any different packaged any other way?"

"This is what I don't know, Papa!" she said, holding her father's mouse paws and gazing up into his face.

The king smiled at his daughter, who seemed to be growing up right before his eyes.

"I do not have a mirror to give you," he finally replied. "It's not that I have anything against mirrors or think it's terrible to see your reflection. I simply would rather you develop a sense of who you are by your heart, and be bothered less by the outside-in. Therefore, I have ordered mirrors not to be present in my kingdom. All the kingdom creatures seem quite happy with this arrangement, but you are less so, my daughter?"

Journee hugged him and kissed his mouse paw. She knew her father was wise, but she needed to find out for herself if his words were true. Then and there she decided on her plan.

"Papa, I love you and know you are wise. I ask that my birthday present be, if not a mirror, your permission to ride out on my birthday, the Saturday next, on a quest to find out who I really am."

With love in his eyes, he said, "my daughter, I grant you my permission to ride out on this grand adventure to discover who you are. I will give you my own mighty steed to guide and protect you on your way. He will watch over you and will bring you home to me when it is time for you to return."

Hearing these words, Journee leaped up into her father's lap and kissed him over and over on his forehead and cheeks, nearly knocking off his crown. He bellowed with laughter, the sound rang throughout the castle, and all nearby could hear the joyful clamor.

Chapter 2
The Quest Begins

The Saturday next finally arrived, and the festivities were about to begin. Every creature throughout the land had come to celebrate Journee's coming-of-age birthday. She emerged from the castle gates, sitting on her father's steed, and greeted the creatures of the realm. But to their great surprise, she announced that instead of celebrating her coming-of-age birthday, she was riding out on a quest to discover who she was. After bidding all farewell, she turned the mighty steed toward the King's High Road. All the creatures waved tentatively in return, feeling a bit disappointed, for they loved parties with goodies and would have much rather been eating cake and celebrating her birthday.

Journee and Mr. Steed traveled far and wide over mountain passes and through deep river gorges. She and the mighty steed rested at night under the fresh-smelling pine trees in the soft grass. Mr. Steed never left Journee's side. He took great pride in being the protector in his role as the king's personal horse. Day turned into night turned into day, until one day they met a toad on the road.

When Journee saw the toad, she gently whispered to her father's steed, "Mr. Steed, promise me you will never reveal to anyone that I am the daughter of the king, for this quest is for me to discover who I am, and I do not wish for any creature to know me as a princess." To which Mr. Steed nodded his head, his mane falling over his eyes.

The toad was green and bumpy, with rather large bulging eyes, and looked altogether unappealing to Journee. She, Mr. Steed, and the toad stared at each other until the toad finally spoke.

"Who are you?" *Ribbit!* "And why do you pass this way?" he croaked.

"Please, sir, my name is Journee, and this is Mr. Steed. I am on a quest to find a mirror to see myself and discover who I am. Do you happen to have a mirror so I can look at my reflection to know how others see me?"

The toad sat there speechless, so Journee continued.

"You see, I was going to celebrate my coming-of-age birthday and realized I didn't fully know myself. I thought finding out what I look like could help."

As she was speaking, she saw the bulging eyes of the toad begin to glisten. Then, much to her surprise, the toad did a very strange thing. He hopped up onto a nearby boulder and started to weep, with large tears dropping from his bulging eyes.

"Oh, my dear Mr. Toad, whatever is the matter?"

Before Journee finished her sentence, she had dismounted in an instant, stood next to him by the boulder, and held his hand in both her own. Mr. Toad let out a mournful croak and shuddered.

"Alas," *ribbit*, he hiccupped, "I wish I could help you, but I do not have a mirror either. By order of the king, no mirrors exist in the realm. You did not know? I thought all creatures were content to know themselves from the inside-out, but now that I see you are not content, it makes me sad." His tears started all over again.

As she tried to comfort him, Journee saw how sensitive and caring he was, and he now did not look disagreeable at all.

Journee squeezed Mr. Toad's hand and kissed away the tears from his cheek. Before she could say anything, however, an owl swooped in from a large tree and landed in front of the boulder.

Whoo-hoo! "I know what you can do-*hoo*," hooted the majestic bird, who had golden, orb-like eyes that never seemed to blink. "Legend has it there exists a beautiful pond of crystal clear water, as smooth as glass, somewhere in the kingdom. It is called the Pond of Reflection because the water remains motionless, offering a perfect reflection of anyone *whoo-hoo* gazes into it."

"This is wonderful," exclaimed Journee, jumping back from the boulder to stand before the owl. "Mr. Owl, can you help me find this Pond of Reflection, so I can gaze into it and see my very own reflection in its waters?"

"Well," *whoo-hoo*, hooted Mr. Owl. "We will need to go on a quest to find it, if this is what you wish to do. I can fly overhead as a scout in the air."

"And I can cover many miles without tiring," said Mr. Steed, who was now approaching the threesome. "I will be your faithful protector against harm." As he said this, he threw his head back and shook his head, allowing his long white mane to tumble over the other side of his strong neck. Mr. Steed was a very handsome horse, with a long white tail and a pale blue hue to his body, which was dappled with brightly colored polka dots.

Clapping her mouse paws, Journee said, "Yes, of course. Mr. Steed is here to protect me and be my guide on my quest to know who I am. He can protect all of us if we continue together!"

Ribbit! croaked Mr. Toad. "I'm coming too! I have never been on a quest before, and it sounds quite daring, adventurous, and maybe even scary at times. But if you are all going, then so will I." And for some reason none could understand, Mr. Toad started to sob once again.

"Mr. Toad, whatever is the matter?" exclaimed Journee, handing him her large handkerchief.

Ribbit, he spluttered. "I've never had friends before, and now I am so happy to be going on a quest with my three new companions." Mr. Toad hiccupped as the others laughed, which then made him cry some more.

"This settles it," exclaimed Journee as she mounted Mr. Steed, pulling Mr. Toad up with her to ride bareback behind her. "Scout on, Mr. Owl. Lead on, Mr. Steed. Together, we continue the quest for the legendary Pond of Reflection, for answers to who I am!"

With these words, Mr. Steed leaped forward at a gallop along the road whence they came, while Mr. Owl swooped into the air and circled above.

All were delighted to be together on a quest—even Mr. Toad felt a new destiny awaited just around the bend.

Chapter 3
River Rage

eighhh! whinnied Mr. Steed, his nostrils flaring as he pulled up with a *snort!* "This doesn't look like a simple river crossing ahead." He slowed to a walk, placing the tip of his hoof on the ground. When he seemed okay, he put the full weight of his hoof down. Step by step, he approached the riverbank. The group had been traveling most of the day, and the sun was now low in the sky.

"We will have to camp here for the night and figure out what we can do in the morning," said Journee. She nimbly dismounted into the tall grass, secretly delighted to hear they were stopping for the night. Mr. Toad tumbled off, bumping into Mr. Steed's side on his way down and landing with a thud. Relieved to feel grass and ground, he rubbed his stiff, numb legs. He hopped about, working to loosen his muscles, and began to turn his attention to dinner. His bulging eyes darted this way and that, hoping for a quick catch of something tasty.

Whoo-hoo! hooted Mr. Owl as he swooped in from above and landed on a boulder in front of Journee.

"Oh," she exclaimed. "Mr. Owl, you startled me. I did not hear you coming because of the river noise. It is flowing brutally fast! How will we be able to cross it?"

Whoo-hoo! Mr. Owl hooted again, his eyes revealing his amusement. "My full apology, my dear Journee. I have scouted the river for a few miles. It is certainly high and swift with runoff from the High Western Mountain this time of year. I think our best chance at crossing it safely is just a short distance downstream, where it narrows and bends considerably."

Neighhh! whinnied Mr. Steed. "No time to worry about it now. I think I will tuck into this tall grass for a spot of supper. It looks delicious." He wasted no time in grazing on a clump and munching with gusto.

Mr. Toad was already busy with his dinner too, jumping after insects and catching them with his long tongue.

"Well," said Journee, "it appears it is up to us to scavenge our dinners, Mr. Owl. I do think I spy some ripe raspberries on the other side of this little meadow. I think I will investigate now." And with that, she hopped out of sight through the tall grass.

Mr. Owl took his cue, flying into the air for a little evening foray. The sun had nearly set, the meadow where they were camped already in shadow. Before long, Mr. Steed, Journee, and Mr. Toad were nestled in for the night, each with their own thoughts about what the day would bring. Mr. Owl would not be joining them until the wee hours of the morning. For he was an owl, after all. The little group knew not to wait up for him. They eventually fell asleep, to the continual rush of the river not far away.

Journee woke up early the following morning to a velvety muzzle against her cheek, followed by a *snort!*

Mr. Steed whinnied in her ear. "Wake up, Princess Journee. We have a big day today crossing this river."

Journee sat up looking around, hoping no one heard Mr. Steed addressing her as a princess. She was relieved to see Mr. Toad still asleep in the grass and Mr. Owl nowhere to be seen.

"You are right, Mr. Steed. It is time to meet this challenge head-on, but hopefully together. Where is Mr. Owl? Still out on his evening foray?"

In response to her question, Mr. Owl swooped in and landed in the center of the little party, causing Journee to jump, and rousing Mr. Toad from his nap.

"Mr. Owl! My goodness, you have a way of startling me. How was your night foray?"

Whoo-hoo! hooted Mr. Owl, eyes wide with amusement. "Very nice, Journee. But the foray has been long over. I have already had my early morning owl nap, then I flew up the course of the river again. I have confirmed our best opportunity to cross safely is at the spot I located yesterday, less than a mile downstream from here. Are we ready?"

Ribbit! "Before breakfast?" hiccupped Mr. Toad. "I would not mind a spot of tea to limber up for the day. But if we must go, we must go." He pulled out the large handkerchief Journee had given him and wiped a few tears from his bulging eyes.

"Oh, my dear Mr. Toad"—Journee laughed—"of course we can have some breakfast. Look, Mr. Steed is grazing now, and I am heading over for more raspberries across the meadow. They are delicious. The sun is rising, so I am sure an insect or two will be in the air for you to snatch soon."

Before Journee could finish, Mr. Toad had already snagged a fly buzzing toward him with his long tongue, both disappearing into his mouth in an instant.

Ribbit! croaked Mr. Toad. "That shall do me nicely until noon, I think!"

They all laughed. After Journee had gathered a few raspberries, she mounted Mr. Steed, pulling Mr. Toad up to sit behind her.

"Let us be off! Lead on, our wise and clever Mr. Owl. We will follow you."

Mr. Owl took flight, careful to stay within sight as Mr. Steed trotted behind their handy scout.

The sun was bright, but it remained crisp and cool by the river. It had not risen high enough to illuminate the far side of the raging tributary. Journee felt a shudder as she contemplated trying to cross to the west side. *Do we really have to cross this river? After all, we have no idea where the Pond of Reflection is*, she thought. For some reason, she knew in her heart more answers to who she was would be found on the far side. She sighed, resolving to cross with her friends.

Whoo-hoo! hooted Mr. Owl. "We are here! The best place to cross this torrent with the hope of reaching the other side."

Mr. Steed slowed to a stop with his charges at the river's edge, investigating the site.

Neighhh! he whinnied. "This is what you call a safe place to cross?" His nostrils flared as he snorted.

"Well, it does have potential," Journee said as she dismounted Mr. Steed, pulling Mr. Toad down with her. "This bend slows the current on our side considerably, and it is shallow. This cuts the distance where the water is deep and fast by at least half, if not more. I agree with Mr. Owl; this is the place to cross whether we like it or not."

Ribbit! croaked Mr. Toad. "I am the best swimmer here, but even I will find it challenging to swim the short distance to the other side where the water is turbulent. Oh, bother, what are we going to do?" He mopped a tear off his cheek, then mopped his entire face.

Whoo-hoo! hooted Mr. Owl. "Not swim, my dear Mr. Toad. Together as a team, we can build a bridge to cross over safely. There are plenty of materials right here for us to-*hoo-hoo* build one."

"What a brilliant idea, Mr. Owl. My, how wise you are," exclaimed Journee.

Neighhh! whinnied Mr. Steed. "I will scout for fallen logs. When I find one, Journee, you can tie it to my harness so I can drag them to the riverside. If we find ones that are long enough, my guess is we will only need three large trunks to span the river."

"I will look for vines for twine," said Journee.

Ribbit! croaked Mr. Toad. "Once we have tied the logs together to make our bridge, I can wade out in the shallow part of the stream to help set it in place."

Whoo-hoo! hooted Mr. Owl. "Once the bridge is in the water, I will fly over to the other side with the twine that is fastened on the far side of the bridge and tether it to the large tree there on the far bank. I think it just might work!"

They all made themselves busy with their tasks.

"Over here, Mr. Steed," Journee called. "Here is a perfect-sized log, both long and wide."

Mr. Toad waved his handkerchief to signal where he and Journee were standing as Mr. Steed strolled up to the pair. He stood as Journee nimbly gathered tree vines to rope the log onto Mr. Steed's harness. Once secure, Mr. Steed began to pull with all his might to drag it to the river's edge. The power it took to do this was impressive, but Mr. Steed did not mind the strain to pull the massive weight of the tree trunk. He was quite proud of his strength and loved the opportunity to prove it to others who were less strong.

Whoo-hoo! hooted Mr. Owl. "Here is another good log for our bridge." He circled overhead and landed in a tree not far from the river, pointing downward with his wing.

The others followed his signal to the spot and delighted in the beautiful specimen Mr. Owl had located.

"This will do nicely," exclaimed Journee. She got to work tying off the log and securing it onto Mr. Steed's harness. He then hauled it the short distance to where the other log was stationed by the river.

They worked straight through half the day without stopping. It felt exciting to be tackling a challenge together as a team, using their unique talents and strengths to solve the problem.

By early afternoon, the group had their log bridge secured end to end, with two exceptionally long ropes at each end for tethering it in place on either side of the river. It was ready to launch into the water, but first, the little crew rested in the grass.

"We are quite the team, to have constructed a log bridge with materials available to us on the landscape." Journee enjoyed another raspberry.

Neighhh! whinnied Mr. Steed. "Yes, Journee, but the real test is coming up. Will this bridge hold up across the water, and if so, will it hold up long enough for all of us to venture across to the other side?" He shook his head, his long mane flopping over his eyes.

Journee knew Mr. Steed all too well and understood that his head shake and mane flopping were a sign of nervousness, though Mr. Steed would never admit to this.

"Oh, my dear Mr. Steed," she said, hopping over to stroke his velvety nose. "I am certain it will hold us simply fine. You more than any of us know how heavy and sturdy these tree trunks are. If we can float it across the river and tie it off on the other end, I think it will last forever and become a passenger bridge connecting the eastern kingdom with the western kingdom. You will see!" She kissed Mr. Steed's nose encouragingly and hopped up onto a boulder.

"Who is ready to cross this river?"

Ribbit! hiccupped Mr. Toad. "I am ready to go with you anywhere, my dear Journee."

Whoo-hoo! hooted Mr. Owl. "Me too-*hoo-hoo!*"

Mr. Steed pawed the soft earth with his hoof.

"All for one and one for all!" he replied, with a snort!

"Alright then," said Journee. "Mr. Owl, help me tether this end of the bridge to this sturdy tree here."

Mr. Owl took the twine rope in his beak and flew several circles around the tree, then made several loops to tie it off and secure it. Nothing would undo that knot. The twine rope would have to break to free the bridge from the tree.

He then picked up the twine rope on the other end of the bridge in his beak and flew across the river to the other side. He would not be able to secure this end until the bridge was across the river. It was now or never. A hushed silence fell over the group.

With great skill, Mr. Toad hopped into the shallow water at the riverbend and waited for Mr. Steed to push the log bridge, with all his might, out and over the riverbank.

Journee hopped up and down, wishing there was something she could do to help, but there was nothing for her to do now but hope. *I wish Papa were with us now*, she thought. She then caught herself in the thought. *I was the one who asked to come on this quest. We will just have to work this out for ourselves.* Journee straightened up a little taller to will some encouragement. For a tiny mouse, Journee was becoming very brave, like her father.

Neighhh! whinnied Mr. Steed. "Pull hard, Mr. Owl! The bridge is halfway across and starting to get caught up in the turbulence closer to your side."

Mr. Owl responded by flying into the air with the twine rope in his beak, heading upstream and away from the bank. It was a struggle, but he was managing to keep his end of the bridge out of the water, for now.

Mr. Toad, now dangerously close to the turbulent river flow where it was deeper, tried to guide the bridge across.

Neighhh! whinnied Mr. Steed. "Lift higher, Mr. Owl, and when you can, tie off your end to the tree not far from you. Make haste. You will not be able to hold that for much longer. It is time. The bridge is in place as best it can be. Tie off, Mr. Owl! Tie off!" Mr. Steed was pawing the riverbank and prancing back and forth, nostrils flared and his mane in wild disarray.

"Oh Mr. Toad and Mr. Owl, do be careful," called out Journee. "If you cannot hold it, let it go! We cannot lose either of you in this effort." Journee mounted Mr. Steed for a better vantage to observe and to call out instructions.

The river roared.

Mr. Steed pranced back and forth with Journee on his back.

Mr. Owl flew with all his might, higher in the air, then began to loop the tether around the grand tree on the riverbank.

Mr. Toad, although now bobbing up and down in the water's turbulence, refused to let go of the bridge until Mr. Owl had safely tied it off.

Standing on Mr. Steed's head, Journee shouted from between his ears, "You have it, Mr. Owl. The bridge is across the river. Secure your side now!"

With a final burst, Mr. Owl made one more loop around the tree and secured his end. He then flopped exhausted on the ground, onto his back, feet up.

Terrified for Mr. Owl, Journee wasted no time dismounting Mr. Steed and grabbing the reins to coax him onto the log bridge. Since navigating slippery wood was not a strong suit for Mr. Steed, Journee knew she would need to encourage him to keep him calm.

"This is it, Mr. Steed. Don't watch the water, only your hooves on the bridge. Easy and gently. If you feel off-balance, stop and gather yourself. Whoa, Mr. Steed, one hoof forward, good, now the other hoof forward. Steady. Gently gather yourself. Good boy. Now one hoof forward, then the other one. Nicely done. Steady. Steady. Mr. Steed, you are halfway across. Take your time. Do not look at the water, watch the bridge. Nicely done."

Mr. Steed shook his head and snorted, but kept his eyes on the bridge.

Journee nudged Mr. Steed across, step by step, slowly and purposefully until one hoof was safely on the west riverbank. Then the other was on

solid soil, then his rear hooves. Mr. Steed lowered his head as Journee hugged his neck, burying her face in his mane and whispering in his ear.

"My father will hear how loyal and brave you have been to me on this journey, Mr. Steed!"

Mr. Steed answered with a *snort!* and a shake of his head.

This time, Journee knew this to signal joy, relief, and pride in himself.

The moment of shared relief was brief, as Journee wasted no time in scurrying over to Mr. Owl, who was now sitting upright a short distance from the bridge but looking quite shaken.

"Oh, my dear Mr. Owl," cried Journee. "You were brilliant. Are you alright? Can I help you?" She took both his wingtips into her mouse paws and held them tightly.

Whoo-hoo! hooted Mr. Owl. "I hope we never have to-*hoo-hoo* do-*hoo-hoo* that again!" he said feebly. Journee laughed and gave Mr. Owl a big squeeze. Then she busied herself propping him up with soft leaves against a log, and sharing her raspberries with him. Mr. Owl eyed these for a minute, then scooped up a mouthful in his beak with gusto.

Mr. Steed had strolled over to the pair and was now interested in munching grass, as if nothing daring or dangerous had happened.

The afternoon was spent, and the sun had dipped behind the ridge not far from them. The meadow was partly in shadow, as the heat of the afternoon ebbed into the cool of the evening.

"Oh!" Journee clambered up onto a rock. "In all the excitement, I forgot about our dear Mr. Toad. He is not here. The last I saw of him he was struggling to steady the bridge in the water." She looked around, but could not see much from her view on the rock. "Oh no! Where could he be?"

The threesome were silent as they collectively realized that Mr. Toad was not with them.

"Oh, my dear Mr. Toad!" Journee sighed as she hopped back toward the riverbank to look for him.

Mr. Owl and Mr. Steed followed. They each looked up the river and down, then across to the other side. Mr. Steed hung his head. He was the protector of the group. How could he lose Mr. Toad in the river?

Indeed, Mr. Toad was nowhere to be found.

Chapter 4
The Enchantment of Whoami Forest

Journee, Mr. Owl, and Mr. Steed stared at the river, speechless. They watched the water for some time. Journee began a silent cry. What would they do and how would they search for her dear friend? After all, it was nearly nightfall.

Little did they know that Mr. Toad, who had been carried downstream a short distance and since had hopped up to the riverbank, had made his way back to the threesome and was sitting behind them. He did not understand why all were so sad, which, of course, made him quite sad too. But it was not until Journee began to cry that he felt the overwhelming

urge to sob himself, which he did, loudly, covering his face with his now-river-soaked handkerchief.

Ribbit! sobbed Mr. Toad. "Oh, this is so sad. Why are you all staring at the river and crying?" He shuddered and blew his nose, causing the others to jump.

"Oh, my dear Mr. Toad. It is you!" Journee hopped over to Mr. Toad, threw her arms around him, and kissed both his cheeks.

Ribbit! he croaked. "Why, of course, it is me. Who else would I be? Why are you so sad?"

Whoo-hoo! hooted Mr. Owl. "We thought we had lost you in the river. We all made it to the other side, but you were nowhere to be found. I must say, even you-*hoo-hoo* are a sight for sore eyes. We are delighted to see you."

Neighhh! whinnied Mr. Steed. "I never thought I would be thrilled to see a toad, but here we all are together, and I am grateful you are here too." Mr. Steed shook his head, his mane falling in his eyes.

Mr. Toad was a bit taken aback at the attention. "Why," he stammered. *Ribbit!* "Just as I saw Mr. Owl secure the bridge on his side of the bank and Mr. Steed step onto the bridge with Journee, I was carried with the current downstream. Instead of fighting the torrent on the other side, I floated with it and soon landed on a boulder. It was easier to hop onto the far bank from there and then find my way back to all of you." *Ribbit!*

"I am glad it happened this way because I could not bear to watch Mr. Steed cross the bridge with his clumsy hooves."

Neighhh! whinnied Mr. Steed. "Clumsy hooves, did you say?" His nostrils flared as he gave a *snort!*

They all laughed. A joyful, wonderful, relieved laugh. The kind of heartfelt laugh that signaled all was well with the world. The little group made their way back to the meadow to camp for the night. Though all were exhausted, none could sleep from the day's excitement. They danced and sang all the adventure songs they knew. They recounted moment by moment their daring feat, and were filled with a sense of accomplishment and success.

Little did they know they were growing increasingly strong and faithful, loving and kind, courageous and wise. Everyone contributed in their unique way to the group, making them together more capable than each alone. Best of all, they were becoming fast friends. And something wonderful happens among friends: the inside-out comes to matter far more than the outside-in.

The next morning dawned bright and cheery. The sun was dazzling, and all were quite happy to be on their way again. This morning was nothing like the previous, where everything was serious and forbidding.

Today was much more carefree, and the adventure to seek out the legendary Pond of Reflection was fun once again.

"Onward, Mr. Steed," shouted Journee, who had mounted him a few seconds before, pulling Mr. Toad up with her. Mr. Owl flew into the air and was circling overhead.

Neighhh! whinnied Mr. Steed. "Delighted to, Pr— I mean, Journee," he replied, shaking his head and snorting at his near-miss at addressing her as a princess.

Before Journee could give a scolding look to Mr. Steed, Mr. Owl interrupted her thought.

Whoo-hoo! "I see a vast forest ahead, not far from here. If a magical Pond of Reflection were to-*hoo-hoo* be anywhere, my guess is it would be somewhere deep within a forest just like the one I see ahead. Shall we head that way, then?"

"Lead on, Mr. Owl!" answered Journee. "I hope we find the Pond of Reflection there. I do want so badly to know who I am from the inside-out and outside-in. I have so much to learn. Do you think the pond is enchanted? It sounds mysterious."

Ribbit! croaked Mr. Toad, already a bit uncomfortable from riding on Mr. Steed's back. "Enchanted or not, I hope I can go for a swim if we do find it!"

"Surely not, Mr. Toad," exclaimed Journee. "Who knows what might happen to you if you swim in an enchanted pool. It might turn you into a fish, and then what would we do with you?"

They all laughed, even Mr. Toad, who was now mopping his brow with his handkerchief. The sun was high now, and it was becoming quite warm.

They rode on for hours. After traveling for a while cross-country, they came to an overgrown road that led them westward in the general direction of the forest. Though this made travel much faster, they could not approach the dense wood quickly enough. It seemed like no time had passed when the sun was dipping behind the High Western Mountain to the northwest, forcing the group to stop for the night.

"This looks like a nice little resting spot, Mr. Steed," said Journee. "Should we turn in here for the evening and start again early in the morning tomorrow?"

Mr. Steed said nothing, but heeded her suggestion and turned off the road into an open meadow, laced with tall green grass and wildflowers. It was a lovely place to bed down for the night.

As always, Mr. Toad tumbled off Mr. Steed's back, stiff and sore, delighted to lie down in the cool shade of the meadow.

Mr. Owl swooped in from above, landing on a nearby log.

Neighhh! whinnied Mr. Steed. "I thought you said the forest was just up ahead, Mr. Owl."

Whoo-hoo! hooted Mr. Owl. "It is just ahead, as the owl flies, that is!"

Mr. Steed snorted, then tucked into supper in the tall grass.

Journee discovered more raspberries and some sunflower seeds, while Mr. Toad snatched a bug or two out of thin air. When the sun had completely set behind the High Western Mountain, the crew—minus Mr. Owl, of course— had already bedded down for a good night's sleep.

Journee hopped up at the crack of dawn, excited to get moving. After gently waking Mr. Toad and Mr. Steed, she encouraged them to have a quick breakfast so they could be on their way. Mr. Owl was not there, which was no surprise to anyone. He would find them on their journey in an hour or two.

"To the forest," called out Journee, who was already on Mr. Steed and prodding him forward. She pulled up Mr. Toad, and regardless of whether they were ready or not, they were off.

"Can we run the road, Mr. Steed?" Journee asked, patting his long mane.

"My pleasure, Journee," whinnied Mr. Steed. In a flash, he was off at a canter, forcing Mr. Toad to hang on to Journee for dear life.

On they went for several more hours. The road by now was less a road than a path, but still quite manageable for Mr. Steed to stretch his legs at a fast clip.

It was not long before Mr. Owl swooped in from overhead and followed the crew just above their heads. The sun was high in the sky when Mr. Owl called out.

Whoo-hoo! he hooted. "We are nearly there. It is just around the bend!"

Mr. Steed allowed himself to slow to an easy trot, then began to walk. Around the bend they came up to a sign that read:

WELCOME TO WHOAMI FOREST

Journee read the sign out loud. "I have never heard of it before, but I guess we have arrived."

Just then, Mr. Owl landed on the back of Mr. Steed behind Mr. Toad to catch a ride. It would be difficult to keep a bird's eye on the traveling companions in the thick of the forest.

Whoo-hoo! "From here on, it is best we all keep together."

Mr. Steed flicked his head to the side at Mr. Owl's landing, but he did not mind. He was hardly any extra weight to carry. The foursome traveled onward in silence. The forest grew dense almost immediately, forcing them to stick to the path. The trees were very tall and almost completely blocked out the sun, creating a surprisingly dark and a bit creepy atmosphere. Only a stray sunray pierced the thick canopy, lighting up the forest floor in scattered patches, here and there.

Mr. Steed continued. The crew felt oddly cut off from the rest of the world. It felt a little oppressive, giving a sense of timelessness. The trees on either side of the path looked ancient, some standing over a hundred feet tall. It was deathly quiet too. There were no sounds of birds, or squirrels, or anything that you would expect to hear in a forest.

"I wonder if this place is enchanted?" whispered Journee. "I feel like the trees are watching us and know why we are here."

Mr. Toad muffled a sob, dabbing his eyes with his handkerchief. "It is a bit odd in here, is it not?"

"Stick with me," whinnied Mr. Steed. "I can protect you in this place."

On they went, keeping to the path going through. It seemed to be the only way to traverse the thickness of the trees. No one dared dismount Mr. Steed, in fear they would be accidentally left behind in this timeless place.

After a long while, Journee spoke up.

"Stop here, Mr. Steed. I have lost all sense of time and we have no sun to guide us. Though I do not know what time it is, I sense it is late, for I am exhausted and hungry. We will stay here for the night and start fresh in the morning. We can step just off the path and lie down in the grass.

*Mr. Owl, I suggest you remain with us tonight,
or we may never find you again."*

Journee dismounted Mr. Steed and hopped over to kiss his nose. Mr. Owl hopped off Mr. Steed's back and swooped to the ground near a tree. Since Mr. Toad was so stiff, he accepted Journee's help dismounting. Glancing around, they looked at each other and swallowed. With encouraging words from each other, they all bedded down for the night, staying close to the path and to each other. They drifted into an uneasy sleep, each to their own uneasy dreams. Morning, if one could tell when it was morning, could not come too soon.

Chapter 5
Who Are You?

*N*eighhhh-choo! sneezed Mr. Steed.

Journee stirred and sat up. "What? What is all of this?"

Whoo-hoo-choo! Mr. Owl followed with a sneeze of his own.

Journee shook her head and watched sparkling yellow pollen float down to the ground.

Mr. Toad was already up and attempting to wring out his handkerchief, now covered in pollen dust.

Looking around, they all gasped. Their camp was now covered, knee-high according to Journee's mouse size, in bright yellow pollen dust.

"Oh, my goodness," exclaimed Journee. "Did the trees do this to us overnight? What a mess; pollen is everywhere, *hee-choo!* We should all shake off the best we can and then get out of here." Journee looked up at the trees standing around them without a hint of pollen dust on them anywhere. "So strange," she mused aloud. "I don't see pollen anywhere

except on our little patch of grass and on all of us. Mr. Steed, are you ready to head out? I think the sooner, the better."

Mr. Steed, however, was in no condition to move. He was lying down having a good sob. Large tears streamed down his cheeks and the bridge of his nose.

Ribbit! croaked Mr. Toad. "Oh, my goodness," he exclaimed. "My dear Mr. Steed, whatever is the matter? I have never seen you cry before, ever! Oh, I am so sorry." He hopped over to Mr. Steed and attempted to stroke his long mane to comfort and encourage him.

Neighhh! whinnied Mr. Steed. "I don't understand it, but a good sob feels like the thing to do. It does seem fitting, does it not? We are lost in a deep, dark forest and now covered with pollen." Another large tear welled up in his eye. "Do you suppose I could borrow your handkerchief, Mr. Toad? I can understand why you love it so."

Mr. Toad granted Mr. Steed's request, for he felt no need to keep it. Mr. Steed took it and blew his nose, which made him sneeze again as the handkerchief was covered in yellow pollen.

"Hmm, this is strange, this!" exclaimed Journee. "Mr. Steed crying? I think you should pull yourself together, Mr. Steed, and let us be off."

They all looked at Journee in surprise. No one had ever heard Journee be stern and matter-of-fact in this manner, especially when Mr. Steed was upset.

"What?" Journee asked, a bit defensively, looking back at the others. "All I am saying is something strange is happening, and I think it would be best to move on from here. Mr. Owl, if Mr. Steed is unable to gather himself together, then I think it wise that you go on ahead to find the best way out of here."

Whoo-hoo! hooted Mr. Owl. "I think I am much better suited to remaining here and protecting the group than scouting an exit. I could never leave the three of you while you are in my care."

Yellow pollen fell from Mr. Owl's tufted ears onto the ground as he refused to budge.

"Since when have you not been delighted to scout for us, Mr. Owl?" Journee replied, a bit taken aback. "It's as if . . . as if . . . ?"

Perplexed, Journee surveyed the group before her, hardly believing what she saw. Mr. Steed was crying into Mr. Toad's handkerchief while Mr. Toad encouraged him. Mr. Owl refused to leave the group because he wanted to protect them, uninterested in scouting a way to safety from the air.

"Oh, my goodness," exclaimed Journee, eyes wide. She hopped onto a boulder to address her friends. "My dear comrades," she began, "I have led you all here because I am on a quest to know who I am, from the outside-in and the inside-out. You are my valiant companions who have never left my side in this adventure. I may not be certain who I am exactly yet, but I certainly have come to know each of you better during this adventure. I think this pollen has enchanted us to act like one another, and our inside-outs do not fit our outsides-in!"

Neighhh! whinnied Mr. Steed. "This is terrible." He began to sob in earnest into Mr. Toad's handkerchief.

"There, there, Mr. Steed." *Ribbit!* "You will be just fine. I just know it," hiccupped Mr. Toad as he patted Mr. Steed's mane.

"My dear Mr. Steed," Journee continued, "you are behaving much like Mr. Toad, with your tears. Mr. Toad, you are behaving more like me, with your encouragement toward Mr. Steed. Mr. Owl, you are behaving like Mr. Steed, who is the protector, by refusing to leave us as a scout. I guess that leaves me being wise like Mr. Owl, considering that I figured this out in the first place."

Whoo-hoo-choo! sneezed Mr. Owl, yellow pollen dust sprinkling down from the top of his head to the ground. "I think you are correct, Journee. How very odd! Why would this ever happen? What does it mean? As much as I admire Mr. Steed, I desire my own self back. I do not have the desire to fly anymore! This is terrible."

Mr. Steed let out another sob at Mr. Owl's words.

Ribbit! croaked Mr. Toad as he continued to console Mr. Steed. "I am starting to get hungry for breakfast. My, this grass looks tasty. I think I'll try some."

While he attempted to pull up a blade or two with his long tongue, he was met without much success. The morsel he did manage to lap up, he immediately spat out.

"Mr. Steed, how do you eat this stuff?"
he croaked, eyes bulging.

Mr. Steed simply shook his head, his long mane flopping over his eyes, spilling pollen dust everywhere.

"Okay, all," Journee said, clapping her mouse paws together and hopping down from the boulder. "To the best of our ability, we need to move on from here and find our way out of this Whoami Forest. Fortunately, there is a single path through, and thus it is the only way we can go."

She looked down the path the way they had come, but it had been closed off overnight with trees. The only way to travel was forward. Journee frowned and shook her head.

"Shall we continue onward?" she said. "I have no sense of time in here. We cannot see the sun or sky, but my tummy tells me it is late morning already. We must make haste! Hopefully, we can find our way out before nightfall."

Journee wasted no time in pulling Mr. Steed up from lying on the pollen-covered ground. Before he could protest, she mounted onto his back, pulling Mr. Toad up with her. Mr. Toad, sensing he was Journee, insisted on riding in front of Journee on Mr. Steed's back and taking the reins. For the sake of getting going, Journee simply shook her head and humored Mr. Toad by settling in behind him.

"Let us be off, Mr. Steed," Journee called out from behind Mr. Toad. "Mr. Owl, try the best you can to fly ahead of us and scout out what lies ahead. We will be fine. You do not need to protect us. We will not stray from the path, and you can check on us often."

Mr. Owl blinked his golden orb-like eyes twice, then lowered his head as he took off into the air. He hung low and flew slowly, wanting instead to remain with the group. Mr. Steed followed Mr. Owl along the path at a kind of half trot, half hop as Mr. Toad tried to manage the reins. He unsuccessfully called out words of encouragement to Mr. Steed, like:

Ribbit! "That's right, Mr. Steed. Doing great," or sometimes, "Looking fine there, Mr. Steed!"

It was an odd spectacle, and no one was happy being forced to be someone other than themself.

Chapter 6
Identity Falls

The foursome struggled the best they could along the path through Whoami Forest. Though surprisingly straight and flat, like a highway, it was only a few feet wide. The flatness of the road made for easy traveling. That is, if your horse did not think he was a toad.

The forest was so dense with trees on either side of the path, it was nearly impossible to step off, even if one wanted to. Forward was the only way to go, which was both comforting and a bit unnerving at the same time.

The loss of a sense of time, space, and identity made the Whoami Forest a very unpleasant place to be, and Journee could not wait to see the back of it. And what about their true characters? *Will we be changed forever?* Journee worried. *Just as I am hoping to figure out who I am in the first place, I lose myself forever?* Shaking this thought out of her head, she remembered the loving words of her beloved Papa instead, which made her feel better.

I think I would love you just as much if you were a rat or a vole or a gerbil, but alas, you are a mouse like me. Do you think your heart would be any different packaged any other way?

"Oh, Papa!" Journee sighed. "We will be fine," she said out loud to the others. "According to my Papa, our hearts are true, and he loves us no matter what!"

Mr. Steed snorted a muffled sob and nodded his head. Mr. Steed knew Journee's beloved Papa well, being the personal steed of the Great Mouse King. Encouraged by these wise words, he nodded his head, partly in agreement with Journee, and partly because Mr. Toad was a terrible driver.

"How about we sing to pass the time?" croaked Mr. Toad. "Remember the adventure songs we sang after our river crossing? We were so happy and victorious then. Let us do it again. The songs will lift our spirits."

Mr. Toad, acting more like Journee with such courage, took the lead and began to sing out loud. They all joined in, even Mr. Owl, who mostly hovered over the group after short scouting forays.

On they went along the path for what seemed like hours and hours. Mr. Steed continued to hop trot along, but the little clan was more joyful now. They had each other. And they were loved by the Great Mouse King, though Mr. Owl and Mr. Toad did not yet know it. They were also moving, slowly but surely, through the Whoami Forest.

Exhausted, Mr. Steed, Mr. Toad, and Journee took one quick break, right on the path. Settled in, Mr. Owl took off for a look ahead. Mr. Toad continued to try and eat grass but never was successful. Resigning himself to being hungry that day, he busied himself cleaning the final remnants of the yellow pollen off Mr. Steed's and his face with the large handkerchief. Try as he could, he could not rub all of it off, and everyone looked like they were stained with yellow dust.

Journee tried to think of something wise to say to the group but was drawing a blank. Her thoughts were interrupted anyway when Mr. Owl flew in and landed right by her.

Whoo-hoo! he hooted. "I cannot quite make it out, but it sounds like a continuously roaring thunder, hardly a mile from here. May I now remain with all of you in case it might be dangerous ahead?"

"Oh," exclaimed Journee, hopping up. "What can it be? Do you think we can get around it, whatever it is?"

Ribbit! responded Mr. Toad. "I guess we will soon find out. Shall we continue?"

They all scrambled to their places, with Mr. Toad remaining in front of Journee to manage (or mismanage) the reins. Mr. Steed hop trotted along the path, trying to keep up with Mr. Owl, who had barely taken flight just overhead. They were off, and hopeful that they were approaching the end of this oppressive place.

"Come to think of it," said Journee to the others, "I don't recall hearing *anything* in this forest the entire time."

Ribbit! stammered Mr. Toad, fumbling with the reins. "I know I have not heard one peep from anything other than us. Not even the sound of a breeze has passed through here. It is most stifling!"

Mr. Steed began to whimper, with a large tear falling down the bridge of his nose.

It was not long, however, until the thunder Mr. Owl warned them about could be heard in the distance.

"We are not far now," Journee called out.

Mr. Owl flew into sight and landed on Mr. Steed's rump behind Journee.

Whoo-hoo! "I think it is a waterfall ahead!"

"Oh my," Journee replied. "That could be a problem."

They continued in silence.

No one spoke as they approached. Actually, no one spoke because it was getting difficult to speak over the thunderous roar.

The path led them onward. Straight. To. The. Waterfall. Then disappeared right through it.

The crew stopped at the beautiful sight. The waterfall cascaded down a rock cliff seventy feet high. There was nothing higher, and a faint rainbow hung just above the start of the fall.

"There is sunshine up there," exclaimed Journee. "Look, a rainbow! You cannot have a rainbow without sunshine."

Neighhh! whinnied Mr. Steed. "But what are we to do now? The path leads right through the waterfall and disappears." His long mane flopped over his eyes as he shook his head and stomped his hoof. A large tear welled up in his eye and slowly made its way down his cheek.

Whoo-hoo! hooted Mr. Owl. "There is a sign over there after all. Perhaps it will tell us what to do?"

"A sign? Where?" asked Journee. "Oh, you are right, Mr. Owl! There is a sign just over here."

She quickly dismounted Mr. Steed and hopped over to it. The others followed, Mr. Toad and Mr. Owl still on Mr. Steed's back. By this point, Mr. Toad had abandoned the reins.

Journee turned the sign for a better look and began to read out loud.

WELCOME TO IDENTITY FALLS
WE HOPE YOU HAVE ENJOYED YOUR STAY IN THE WHOAMI FOREST.

Journee paused and looked at the others, who looked astounded.

Ribbit! croaked Mr. Toad. "Is not the word *enjoyed* overdoing it a bit?"

Journee looked back at the sign and continued.

> IF YOU HAVE NOT DISCOVERED BY NOW,
> WHOAMI IS FOREST LANGUAGE FOR
> WHO AM I?
> DO YOU KNOW WHO YOU ARE?

Journee paused again and hung her head slightly. *This is the reason I have journeyed here. To find out who I am!* She began reading again.

> PERHAPS BY NOW, AT LEAST, YOU KNOW WHO YOU ARE NOT?
> YOU HAVE DISCOVERED IDENTITY FALLS BECAUSE
> YOU HAVE PASSED THE WHOAMI TEST OF CHARACTER:
> TO KNOW WHO YOU ARE NOT,
> WHICH IS HALFWAY TO KNOWING WHO YOU ARE.
> YOU MUST EXIT THIS FOREST, NOW.
> THERE IS ONLY ONE WAY OUT:
> THROUGH THE IDENTITY FALLS.
> GOODBYE. AND THANK YOU FOR COMING!

The little group stared at the sign. Identity Falls was booming ahead of them. Journee reread the sign to herself, certain she had misread something. The words were clear, however. *There is only one way out: Through the Identity Falls.*

Journee turned to look up at the falls, then dipped a toe in the quiet pool of water at her feet. It felt refreshing. She looked back at the sign, then to the others, who were all staring back at her with wide eyes. She turned back to look at the falls again.

"We have to go through," she said wisely.

Ribbit! croaked Mr. Toad. "That is okay. We will do it together," he encouraged.

Whoo-hoo! hooted Mr. Owl. "I can go first. The protector always goes first."

Behind Journee's back, she could hear Mr. Steed attempt to stifle a quiet sob.

Chapter 7
The Only Way Is Through

Neighhh! whinnied Mr. Steed. "If it is time we exit this strange place, at least we will do it with a swim through the falls." He shook his head and attempted to clear the tears from his eyes, collecting himself.

"Mr. Steed," replied Journee, "you hate water, especially if there is a current!"

Ribbit! spluttered Mr. Toad. "Mr. Steed likes the water, Journee, because he is currently me and I am him, and I can tell you, I do not want to go in."

"It is the only way, Mr. Toad," Journee said matter-of-factly. "We all ride on Mr. Steed's back, and we go through it together. Perhaps the fact that Mr. Steed is not afraid of the water now works to our advantage. He will take us through, and the rest of us must hang on tightly. Are we ready? We have no time to waste! We either go through now, or we sit here in this formidable place until we decide to go through anyway."

Surprised at her wisdom and her lack of empathy for the others, Journee shrugged. *I guess this is the owl way.*

Without waiting for a response, Journee hopped back onto Mr. Steed to join the others. This time, she insisted on sitting in the front so she could be in control of the reins. *Mr. Steed might enjoy water now, but it will be tricky walking him through a waterfall.* Mr. Toad relented, now sandwiched between Journee and Mr. Owl. Journee eased Mr. Steed into the pool of water, steering him toward Identity Falls.

Step by step, they waded in the cool, refreshing pool, which never seemed to deepen, remaining shallow.

As they approached, the falls were deafening. Mr. Steed held up, but Journee prodded him onward.

"This is it, Mr. Steed," Journee yelled in his ear. She could barely hear herself over the din. The water was more turbulent here, and it frothed at Mr. Steed's hooves.

Ribbit! croaked Mr. Toad. "Hang tight, Mr. Steed. You will be fine! Just walk forward and through," he called out.

Journee felt Mr. Toad squeezing her shoulders as they all prepared for the massive power of the waterfall.

"This is it, Mr. Steed. Two more paces and we will be under the fall then through. You can do it!"

Mr. Steed gave a loud *snort!* after inhaling the water spray in his flared nostrils. He then gritted his teeth and walked forward. One hoof forward. Steady. Second hoof forward. Steady. One hoof . . .

"What? What happened?" cried out Journee. "We are here? On the other side? But I barely felt a light mist on my face."

Whoo-hoo! hooted Mr. Owl. "We have indeed passed through," he said, "and I am in need of stretching these beautiful wings of mine a little bit!" Mr. Owl then took off from Mr. Steed's rump and made circles above the crew, gaining speed, and circling higher and higher in the air.

Neighhh! whinnied Mr. Steed. "Mr. Toad, my full apology. You can have your handkerchief back." He took the handkerchief between his teeth and flung it back to Mr. Toad, who accepted it gratefully.

Ribbit! croaked Mr. Toad, hugging the handkerchief. "I have missed you so much," he sobbed. "How could I possibly lose you?"

He tumbled off Mr. Steed's back into the pool of water the horse was still standing in after passing through the falls. "The water is perfect. I think I shall enjoy a little swim." He proceeded to jet out into the pond, catching flying insects with his long tongue and rolling them both up into his mouth. "Oh, is it not wonderful to be alive? What a glorious day."

As Mr. Toad dove in, Journee turned back to look at the waterfall they had just passed through. It was a slim ribbon of water trickling down the rock cliff on this side. It gave a soothing sound as it gently entered the pool below it. She then turned back to Mr. Steed and led him over to the bank and, once on dry land, dismounted. She rubbed Mr. Steed's nose affectionately and then kissed it.

"Oh," she exclaimed, "Mr. Steed, you are completely clean! There is not a hint of yellow on you anywhere!"

Neighhh! whinnied Mr. Steed. "And the same for you, Princess Journee," he said so only she could hear.

"Does this? Does this mean? Do we have our identities back, do you think?"

"Well," Mr. Steed replied, "let us see. Mr. Owl is off stretching his wings on a nice foray, and Mr. Toad is delighting in both his handkerchief and a swim. You seem very much like your princess self, and I feel fit as a fiddle and cannot wait for some green grass before a long canter to stretch these legs."

"Then we are back to our normal selves," exclaimed Journee. "This is wonderful! This must be why the falls are called Identity Falls. The only way to leave Whoami or Who-Am-I forest, which swaps your identity with your companion, is to go through Identity Falls to get your true self back."

Neighhh! Mr. Steed whinnied through a long blade of grass dangling from his mouth. "What a strange place, Whoami Forest. I wonder what it is all about and for how long it has been enchanted?"

"I do not know," replied Journee, sprawling out in the sunshine on the pool's bank. "All I know is that I am on a quest to discover who I am. And remember what the sign read?"

YOU HAVE DISCOVERED IDENTITY FALLS BECAUSE
YOU HAVE PASSED THE WHOAMI TEST OF CHARACTER:
TO KNOW WHO YOU ARE NOT,
WHICH IS HALFWAY TO KNOWING WHO YOU ARE.

Perhaps the Whoami Forest made itself available to us to help me discover who I am. At least now I know I am not like Mr. Owl, though I love him dearly."

Neighhh! whinnied Mr. Steed. "And I know I am not like Mr. Toad, though I don't mind at all being in his company!"

Just then, Mr. Toad hopped onto the bank from the water to join Journee and Mr. Steed. The moment he joined the others he sat down, lifted his head, and croaked a gigantic sob.

"Oh, my dear Mr. Toad, whatever is the matter?" Journee exclaimed, taking his wet hand into both of her mouse paws.

Ribbit! he hiccupped. "It is just that I feel so wonderful being me, so I just have to enjoy a good sob!"

Mr. Steed shook his head, hair flopping over his eyes, as he munched on more grass.

Then, slowly, one by one, each could not hold it in any longer, and they all enjoyed a good laugh.

Chapter 8
Full Circle?

Mr. Owl was obviously enjoying himself, for he still had not returned to the group by early evening. This side of Identity Falls was beautiful and a perfect place to camp for the night.

Journee discovered an abundance of raspberries, seeds, and nuts. The pool of water was very refreshing to dip in, and Mr. Toad and Mr. Steed both found plenty to eat in flying insects and grass.

They sat together, enjoying each other's company late into the night. They watched the moon rise over the ridge and marveled at how wonderful it was to see the sky and feel the breeze. They all agreed Whoami Forest may have taught them some lessons, but it was a place they hoped to never visit again. They also laughed at how funny each of them had been, trying to be like the other. Even Mr. Toad ribbed Mr. Steed.

Ribbit! he croaked, with a wide grin. "I think you look quite handsome when you cry, Mr. Steed, and perhaps you should try and do it more often!"

Neighhh! whinnied Mr. Steed, nostrils flaring. "I don't expect to be needing your handkerchief anytime soon, Mr. Toad!" Mr. Steed cocked his head to one side, looking sideways at him. "I think my favorite time in Whoami Forest was watching you try to eat grass, my dear Mr. Toad!" *Neighhh!* Mr. Steed whinnied a laugh as he good-naturedly poked fun.

Journee laughed at the two of them. "I actually thought it felt good to be as wise as Mr. Owl for once, but I do not miss being quite so matter-of-fact without thinking how others might feel."

They nestled down next to each other and pondered their own thoughts before they fell fast asleep in the warm sand by the pool. It was so nice to be out of Whoami Forest and to at least know who they were not, while being happy to be back to who they were. Even if they were not quite certain who that was.

The next morning, when the group awoke to the most glorious sunrise, Mr. Owl was surprisingly already there waiting for them.

Whoo—hoo! he hooted. "Finally, you are up, you sleepy heads!"

"What is it, Mr. Owl?" Journee asked, sitting up and yawning. "Did you enjoy your evening?"

Whoo-hoo! he hooted. "I certainly did, Journee. But I have some news for all of you."

"Good news or bad news?" Journee responded.

"That depends," replied Mr. Owl.

"Oh," Journee exclaimed, hopping up with much more attention. "What is it, then?"

Whoo-hoo! hooted Mr. Owl, eyes wide and a bit mischievous. "It is a matter of where exactly we are."

Ribbit! croaked Mr. Toad. "Will you tell us, or do we have to guess? Are we still in the Whoami Forest, and all this is yet another enchantment? I rather like this one, if we are."

Whoo-hoo! hooted Mr. Owl. "No, we are not back in Whoami Forest, but we are on the east side of the river we had to so daringly cross in the first place to get over to the western part of the kingdom. And as a matter of fact, I discovered in last night's foray that we are not all that far from where we all met and began this adventurous quest of ours."

"Wha-a-a-t?" stammered Journee. "Are you telling us that after all this time and effort we have landed ourselves full circle?" Journee sat back down on the sand, looking as if she might cry. "Oh, dear me!" she sighed.

Neighhh! whinnied Mr. Steed. "I have come on this journey to protect you, all of you, and if we have to start again, then we start again." Mr. Steed stood up tall, looking very loyal and proud when he said this.

Whoo-hoo! hooted Mr. Owl. "Cheer up, my dear Journee. Remember, we do not know where the Pond of Reflection is or if it exists at all. For all we know, it could be farther east than west and thus we are still on the right track."

Journee was not quite following Mr. Owl's reasoning, but it made her feel a bit better anyway.

"In fact," Mr. Owl continued, "if the Pond of Reflection is not to be found out west, then I have a hunch where it might be, possibly more south and east, toward the kingdom palace, though still a journey from the palace itself."

Mr. Steed and Journee glanced at each other, but said nothing.

"Well, I guess we follow your hunch, Mr. Owl, and we head southeast from here. Whether we find the Pond of Reflection or not, it would feel nice all the same to be heading in that direction."

She glanced again at Mr. Steed, who looked down, acting interested in a blade of grass. Journee did not mention that heading southeast would bring them closer to the king's palace *and home* for her.

"Shall we be off, then?" Journee said, feeling much better than when she first heard they had trekked full circle.

"Wait a minute," Journee said. "Why can't I just look at my reflection in this pool of water and forgo finding the Pond of Reflection? The pool water was much too turbulent on the other side of Identity Falls, but possibly here on this side?"

Journee hopped over to the pool's edge and looked in.

"Oh, dear. The pool is much too murky to see anything!" She resigned herself to keep looking for the Pond of Reflection for answers to her questions.

After a scrumptious but hasty breakfast, Journee mounted Mr. Steed, pulling Mr. Toad up behind her. She called out to Mr. Owl as he swooped into the air and circled above.

"Lead on, Mr. Owl. You are our scout and our guide. We will follow you!"

As Mr. Steed leaped forward with his charges, Journee thought to herself how wonderful it was to have her friends back. It was nice having a steed, a toad, and an owl as her companions, and nice that they behaved exactly how they each should behave accordingly. After all, each contributed their God-given talents to the group, and they were better for it. There is nothing to be done with a horse who cannot run, an owl who is reluctant to fly and scout, or a toad who wants nothing to do with water.

"There is a purpose and a reason to why and how each of us are made," Journee said to no one in particular as they strode along.

"I do not know how it is so, but this realization is very comforting to me!"

Mr. Steed nodded his head in agreement, and Mr. Toad pulled out his handkerchief and blew his nose.

"What a wonderful thing to say, Journee!" He hiccupped and sobbed into his handkerchief.

Journee had a sense that, though they were near where they had started their journey together, they had come a long way, and they had each grown up considerably from when their quest began.

Chapter 9
The Pond of Reflection

The crew rode for two days. They relaxed and enjoyed themselves. They quit early and camped long so Mr. Owl could enjoy his forays way into the night. The weather was delightful, with summer in full season by now. Raspberries were everywhere, flowers, brooks, meadows, and canyons. Another beautiful sight was the High Western Mountain to the northwest. It was the highest point in the kingdom and loomed large in the distance. Just to the west of it was the ocean, and to the north resided the Great Plains. It was a wondrous place to be and to share with best friends.

Journee had never known so much of her father's kingdom before and was enjoying it with her companions, especially Mr. Steed. It was nice to have his loyalty in her little secret that she was a princess, daughter of the Great Mouse King himself.

They were all quite content to take a break from the high demands of crossing raging rivers and losing oneself in the Whoami Forest.

While they were strolling along on Mr. Steed, Mr. Owl called out from above.

Whoo-hoo! he hooted. "There it is!"

"Oh," exclaimed Journee. "Where what is? The Pond of Reflection?"

Whoo-hoo! laughed Mr. Owl. "No, my dear Journee, the rock where you met Mr. Toad and I swooped in and told you about the Pond of Reflection in the first place."

Mr. Steed leaped forward at a canter with his charges. They were now on the familiar King's High Road and easier traveling again. He slowed to a stop at the familiar boulder as Mr. Owl swooped in from above, landing on top of it.

Journee and Mr. Toad dismounted Mr. Steed. Mr. Toad hopped over to the boulder and touched it reverently with his hand. He then pulled out his handkerchief and began to cry.

Ribbit! "This is where my life changed forever!" he sobbed. "I will remember this rock fondly for the rest of my life."

They gathered around the boulder and decided to have a picnic there, relaxing and marveling at all that had happened since they had been there.

"I think we should call it for the day and just enjoy ourselves here until tomorrow," suggested Journee. "What do you all think?"

Neighhh! whinnied Mr. Steed. "Excellent idea! I think I just might have myself a good roll in this soft grass over here." He headed straight for it, then plopped down and rolled onto his back, four hooves in the air.

The others laughed and joined in with their own relaxing activities.

They had the most marvelous time, telling stories and sharing their experiences of where they were from and what led them to the spot where they all met. Though Journee was careful not to disclose she was a princess or where exactly she lived, she shared lots of wonderful stories.

They nestled in together and slept under what appeared to be a full moon. It was a happy time together. There was no question that they had become the absolute best of friends.

The next morning, they were up with the sunrise, refreshed and ready to push on.

Mr. Toad touched his boulder one last time to say goodbye before Journee pulled him up behind her onto Mr. Steed's back.

Mr. Owl swooped into the air as he called out to them below.

Whoo-hoo! he hooted. "We are heading south from here. There is a canyon not far as the owl flies from here. Whoo-*hoo* knows? The Pond of Reflection could be in that canyon!"

He was heading higher in the sky, when Journee called after him.

"Lead on, Mr. Owl. We are right behind you."

After many hours, Mr. Owl hooted from above.

Whoo-hoo! "I think I see it! There is a deep gorge straight ahead, with what might be a pond at the very bottom!"

Mr. Steed leaped ahead and, on reaching the gorge, guided them down the long steep slope to its base. From there, they made slow progress, for the gorge was rather dark and filled with large, leafy trees blocking the brilliant sunshine above. After some time, the narrow gorge walls began to widen into a grassy, overgrown clearing. Through tall weedy grass and leafy trees, Mr. Steed finally brought them to the pond's edge. The water was as smooth as glass and sparkled brilliantly when a sunray happened to strike the surface through the deep, overgrown ravine. The air was still and silent, rendering the place timeless and mysterious.

Journee dismounted and discovered a small sign half-covered by reeds. Mr. Owl swooped down and, landing on her shoulder, read the sign aloud.

POND OF REFLECTION

PONDER YOUR REFLECTION TO REFLECT ON YOUR HEART WITHIN

"Oh, we have found the legendary Pond of Reflection!" Journee exclaimed.

Still sitting on Mr. Steed's back, Mr. Toad was so excited at these words that he started to cry, dabbing in quick succession at his bulging eyes with his handkerchief.

Whoo-hoo! hooted Mr. Owl. "How exciting. But do you think it is safe to peer into the water? It is enchanted. What if we all look and turn into statues or something worse? Legends are legendary for a reason: they have passed down through generations and remain mysterious and unexplainable, with dangerous details potentially lost in passage."

Journee had been worrying. *What could possibly be worse than turning into a statue*? But before she could say something, Mr. Toad cut into her thought.

Ribbit! "What? We have come all this way to find the legendary Pond of Reflection, and now that we have, you suggest we not peer into this crystal clear body of water? It looks so inviting that I might not only look but dive in for a swim!"

And with these words, Mr. Steed stomped his hoof in agreement, inadvertently bumping Mr. Toad off his back and onto the ground, prompting laughter from them all.

Neighhh! "I agree with Mr. Toad. We must finish the quest. Journee should peer into the Pond of Reflection first. It is for this very moment I have journeyed with her all this way: for her to discover who she is."

"Let us all look at the same time!" replied Journee. "Who is ready to peer into the Pond of Reflection with me?"

"I am!" whinnied Mr. Steed.

"Me too!" croaked Mr. Toad.

"I guess then I'm ready too-*whoo-hoo!*" hooted Mr. Owl.

After a glance at each other, the friends leaned over the water together.

"Oh!" they exclaimed in unison, as they marveled at their reflections. They stared into the water for quite some time until Journee finally spoke, almost in a whisper.

"I see my father's likeness from the outside-in, for I am a mouse, small and furry, with round ears and a pointy nose, just as my father is a mouse and just as he told me I was. But unlike him, my fur is lighter brown, while my father's is a darker gray. But still, I am a mouse like him all the same."

Whoo-hoo! hooted Mr. Owl. "I see an owl staring back at me. I have round golden eyes, a sharp curved beak, and glossy brown feathers." *Whoo-hoo!* "And, thankfully, I haven't turned into a statue, but remain a living, breathing owl."

Mr. Steed could not look away from the water. He saw a handsome, strong, and brave member of the king's court, just as he knew he was in his heart. He was very content to be a horse.

As Mr. Toad looked closely at his reflection in the still water, his bulging eyes began to mist and glisten. Then, before he could say *ribbit*, big teardrops began to flow down both cheeks and into the water. As if by magic, his tears landing in the Pond of Reflection did not make a ripple or ring. The water remained smooth as glass.

"Oh, my dear Mr. Toad," exclaimed Journee. "Whatever is the matter?"

Mr. Toad looked up at the three of them, and with watery eyes exclaimed, "I see myself as green and bumpy, with big bulging eyes, so altogether disagreeable!" And with these words, the tears fell in earnest.

Journee rushed over to Mr. Toad, held his hand, and peered with him into the Pond of Reflection.

"Oh, Mr. Toad, when I gaze into the pond and see your reflection, I see a toad who is the kindest friend I have ever had. Your reflection is beautiful to me, for I know your heart is sensitive and caring."

She dabbed his tears away with the large handkerchief she had given him as they both laughed together. Suddenly, she recalled the words her father had spoken to her in the throne room:

I simply would rather you develop a sense of who you are by your heart and be bothered less by the outside-in.

Oh Papa, she thought, *you were right all along! The outside-in is just not as important as who we are from the inside-out.* More words from her father came back to her as she continued looking at their reflections:

Ah, I think I would love you just as much if you were a rat or a vole or a gerbil, but alas, you are a mouse like me. Do you think your heart would be any different packaged any other way?

"Oh my," Journee exclaimed, interrupting the others' reveries, as they were all still gazing into the Pond of Reflection. "I now know who I am, from the inside-out as well as the outside-in, and my father was right. I should have known he would be. Everyone says he is a wise king."

"Your father is the king?" *Ribbit!* "As in the king of the entire realm? You never told us! This means you are not only a mouse but a princess too, and still you like me as a friend?" stammered Mr. Toad as he began to cry.

Whoo-hoo! Mr. Owl exclaimed. "I never thought I would share adventures with a daughter of a king!"

"Shush!" Journee gently chided as she continued.

"What do we all see when we gaze into the Pond of Reflection? We see a mouse, a toad, an owl, and a horse, but when I inspect your reflections, I see much more in you than this. Mr. Toad, I see less a toad than a sensitive, kind friend. Mr. Owl, I see less an owl than a thoughtful, wise companion, and Mr. Steed, I see less a handsome horse than my protector who is strong, courageous, faithful, and loyal."

Neighhh! whinnied Mr. Steed. "Less a handsome horse, did you say?" And they all laughed until Journee raised her hand to silence them as she continued.

"Also, what I see in the water is my father's likeness, a mouse on the outside. But I also see what I know to be true in my heart: I am loving, encouraging, and adventurous too. I know myself from the inside-out as well as the outside-in!"

They all cheered and then continued to marvel at and ponder their reflections in this legendary water.

"My dear friends, Mr. Toad and Mr. Owl"—Journee turned to them— "I am ready to return home to my father, but it would break my heart to part from you after this wonderful journey we have taken together. Would you come home with me to my father's palace? He would love to meet my loyal friends."

"We would be delighted!" they both chimed in at once.

"Wonderful," Journee exclaimed as she mounted Mr. Steed, pulling up Mr. Toad behind her. "Let us be off like the wind toward home!"

Chapter 10
Homeward Bound!

Once they had navigated their way out of the box canyon where the Pond of Reflection resided and were back on the King's High Road, Mr. Steed leaped to a canter toward the east. He carried Journee and Mr. Toad over mountains and meadows toward the king's palace and home, while Mr. Owl flew above them. Day rolled into night rolled into day, until finally the king's palace could be seen on the horizon. With a *snort!* Mr. Steed crossed the final pasture and cantered with his charges through the palace gates into the king's throne room. He lowered Journee off his back before the throne, never leaving her side. Mr. Toad tumbled off, his legs a bit stiff, for as always, the ride had been rough and not to his liking. Mr. Owl swooped in seconds behind Mr. Steed and landed next to Journee. All bowed. This time, Mr. Toad did all he could not to cry.

After affectionately greeting his mighty steed, the king looked a long time at this dignified little group and then at his daughter, with great love in his eyes. He finally spoke. "My daughter, did you find what you were seeking?"

"Papa, we had the most amazing adventure! I met my two friends, Mr. Toad and Mr. Owl, along the road far from here, and they joined me and Mr. Steed to help me succeed in my quest to discover who I am. And after many days and adventures through Whoami Forest and Identity Falls, we found the Pond of Reflection. I now know who I am inside and out, and together, I think we have hearts like yours: good and kind, wise and courageous, and—"

"My daughter"—he kissed her mouse paw and beamed at her friends—"take a deep breath and calm yourself. I understand how excited you are, for I, too, went on a quest a long time ago, when I was just about your age, and I, too, found these places and the Pond of Reflection.

"Oh Papa, really? You discovered the Pond of Reflection?" Journee excitedly interrupted her father, and then fell silent. It had been a while, and she was rusty on throne room protocol and correct manners.

"It was there I discovered that the outside-in is less important than knowing the heart from the inside-out," her father continued. "Creatures come in all sizes and packages, but it is the heart within that matters. At the Pond of Reflection, I realized my heart was good, kind, courageous, and wise. My daughter, you have done well. You now know who you are. And hmm, did you discover your heart to be loving, encouraging, and a bit adventurous too? Bravo!" he exclaimed with delight.

The king jumped up and called for his attendants. Three courtiers entered and bowed before the king. After a brief and private discussion with them that the others could not hear, they left. Soon the attendants returned, the first with a robe and crown, the second with a beautiful gemstone, and the third with three gold medallions. The king signaled for his daughter to kneel before him. He draped the robe over her shoulders, then placed the crown on her head.

"This crown," said the king, "is the coming-of-age gift I had intended to give you on your birthday."

He then took the precious gemstone and held it reverently in his hands.

"This gemstone, however, you have earned with your courage. It honors your loving heart, adventurous spirit, and your pursuit of self-discovery."

After placing the gemstone in the center of her crown, he stepped back to admire his daughter. *How regal and grown-up you are, my daughter,* he thought.

The king then called Mr. Steed, Mr. Toad, and Mr. Owl to stand before him. He hung a gold medallion around each of their necks and knighted them for their faithfulness to his daughter and their courage on this quest.

Turning to his daughter and his faithful steed, he said with a twinkle in his eye, "Go and celebrate this day with all your friends, great and small!"

She bowed to her father while kissing his mouse paw, then mounted Mr. Steed and rode out of the throne room. Horse and rider greeted the throng that had gathered in the palace courtyard to welcome her return. They saw Journee wearing the beautiful robe and crown, and marveled at her poise and regal bearing.

"Hail the daughter of the king. She has returned home to us!" they cheered.

Chapter 11
A Belated Birthday Celebration

All cheered again as the king and his courtiers, followed by Mr. Toad and Mr. Owl, joined them in the courtyard with a giant cake. The coming-of-age birthday celebration had finally begun! Mr. Toad, overwhelmed with joy to be in a palace eating birthday cake with his friends, began to cry.

It was a momentous occasion. They celebrated Journee's and Mr. Steed's safe return from their quest. They celebrated Journee's coming-of-age birthday, albeit rather belatedly. They celebrated Journee's new friends, Mr. Toad and Mr. Owl, her growing maturity, her newfound confidence, and their own unique and generous hearts. The jubilation carried on well into the night, with toasts, dancing, and singing. Even Mr. Toad could not stop smiling and laughing, for he was beginning to sense how special and valued he was. *Who needs a mirror when you are loved for your heart?* he thought.

Ribbit! he croaked. "I see that all the creatures feel special too, for look how happy they are as they celebrate with their beloved king and his court."

Neighhh! whinnied Mr. Steed as he came up behind Mr. Toad, with Mr. Owl riding happily on his back. "Beloved king, did you say? Yes, we love our king, for he makes each of us feel appreciated for who we are."

Before Mr. Steed could say anything more, he was interrupted by a gong, as the king hopped up onto a table and lifted his glass in the air. The crowd fell silent, listening as the king spoke.

"I propose a toast to my daughter, Journee. On a quest of self-discovery, she overcame many challenges along with her friends, found the Pond of Reflection, and learned a significant truth. This truth of life has meaning for all of us in this kingdom:

As water reflects the face, so one's life reflects the heart."

All drank the toast to Journee as she hugged her three friends, Mr. Steed, Mr. Owl, and Mr. Toad. She then led them into the crowd to join the celebration.

In a kingdom where the inside-out matters more than the outside-in, and all are considered special by a wise and caring king, there are always occasions for celebration, joy, laughter, and of course, cake!

Acknowledgements

Special thanks to:

Illustrator Brooke Connor, of Brooke Connor Design LLC, whose remarkable talent brings storytelling to life. Editor Katie Chambers of Beacon Point LLC, whose professional eye polished this work and made it shine. You have been a fun teacher and a life saver. Thank you, proofreader Leona Skene of Intuitive Editing, formatter Janell E. Robisch of Speculations Editing, marketing consultant Gia Wittmann of Virtual Perfect Assistant, and mentor Ellaine Ursuy of Self-Publishing School! You are each superb professionals as well as super fun to work with.

An author might have an inspiration for a story, but it takes a professional village to publish a book.

About the Author & Illustrator

Author Catherine (Cat) Ann Russell

Catherine (Cat) Ann Russell, moved to action in 2019 to address the infant and child famine crises in Yemen, wrote and published children's books to support organized emergency famine relief efforts through her Basketful Relief Project (www.basketfulreliefproject.com). She has written three children's picture books, *Get to Bed!, The Little Book of Why,* and *Picco and Wren Three*. From there, she wrote a children's chapter book series, The Pearls of Wisdom Series: Stories Inspired by a Biblical Proverb: *The Pond of Reflection, The Hyrax Song,* and *The Zoe-Chai Seed*. In 2002, she started her own digital multimedia company called Spike Productions (www.spikeproductions.com), after a career as a professional research scientist at the National Oceanic Atmospheric Administration (NOAA). Cat lives in Lyons, Colorado, on a small farm with her husband, Ed, and several farm animals, including two burros named Nikki and Norman.

Illustrator Brooke Connor

Brooke Connor of Brooke Connor Design (www.brookeconnordesign.com) lives and works in Boulder, CO. She retired from a career as an environmental chemist after 28 years of left-brained activities, and now is a full-time right-brained illustrator. Brooke specializes in alcohol marker illustrations of birds and wildlife. Her style can be described as extremely colorful, imaginative, and whimsical. Other publications include works with her friend and author, Patricia Kittelson, including, *Bixley Baines and the Beehive Fence, Bixley Baines and the Recycled Crayons, A Kid's Guide to Bryce Canyon,* and *Cedar Breaks for Kids.*

Books by Catherine Ann Russell

Basketful Relief Project (BRP)

Children's Picture Books

Get to Bed!
The Little Book of Why
Picco and Wren Three

Children's Chapter Books

The Pearls of Wisdom Series: Stories Inspired by a Biblical Proverb

Book 1: The Pond of Reflection
Book 2: The Hyrax Song
Book 3: The Zoe-Chai Seed

All books available soon in various formats by the end of the year, 2021 and 2022.

CPSIA information can be obtained
at www.ICGtesting.com
Printed in the USA
LVHW070456011221
704699LV00004B/43